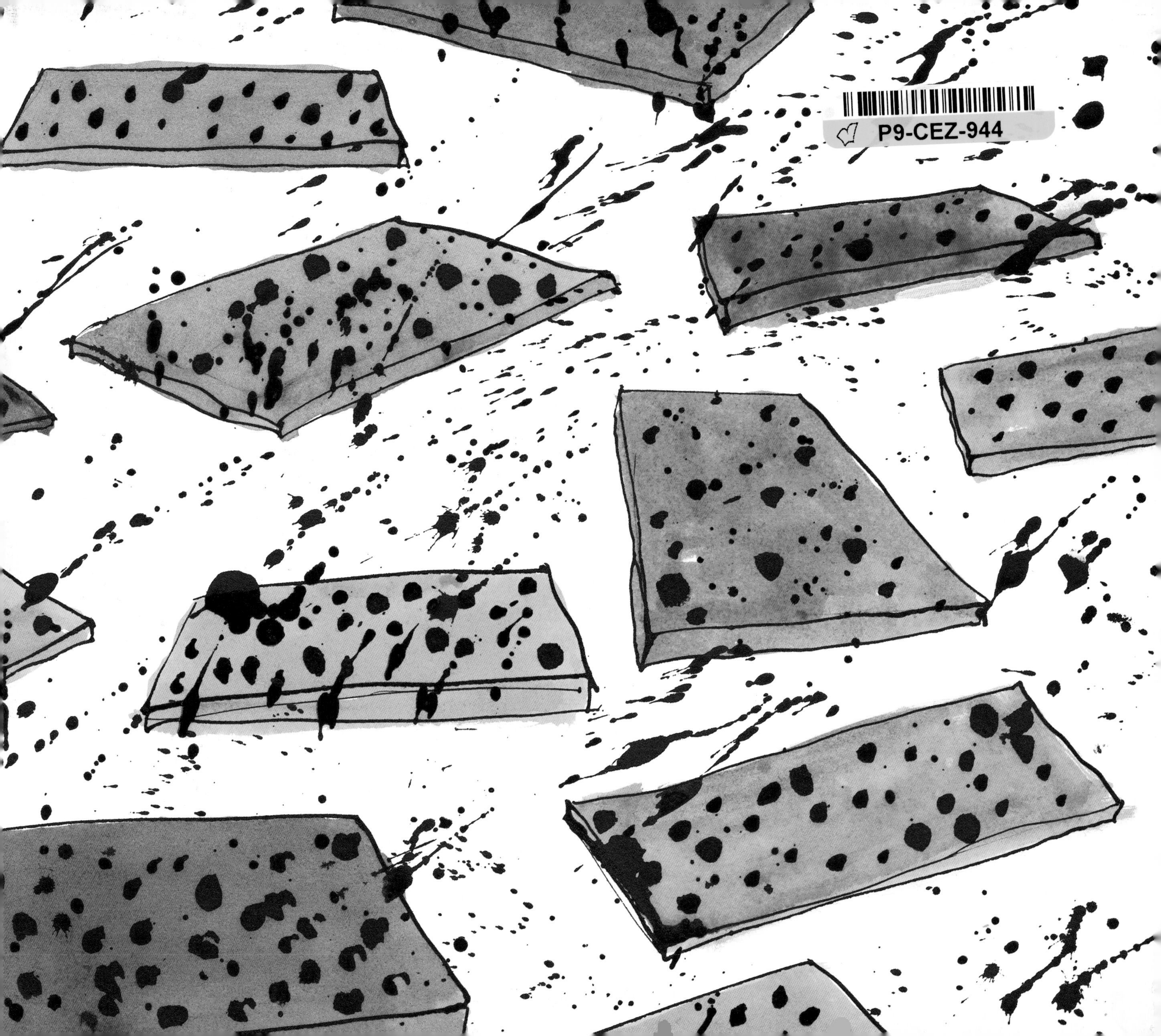

For Barbara and Marcello

First published by Andersen Press Ltd., London
First Marshall Cavendish edition, 2009

Marshall Cavendish Corporation
99 White Plains Road, Tarrytown, NY 10591
www.marshallcavendish.us/kids

Library of Congress Cataloging-in-Publication Data
Steadman, Ralph.
Garibaldi's biscuits / written and illustrated by Ralph Steadman. — 1st Marshall Cavendish ed.
p. cm.
Summary: In nineteenth-century Italy, the wife of General Garibaldi bakes biscuits, as a peace offering, for the defeated French army.
ISBN 978-0-7614-5578-3
1. Garibaldi, Giuseppe, 1807-1882—Juvenile fiction. [1. Garibaldi, Giuseppe, 1807-1882—Fiction. 2. Generals—Fiction. 3. War—Fiction. 4. Biscuits—Fiction. 5. Italy—History—1789-1870—Fiction.] I. Title.
PZ7.S809Gar 2009
[E]—dc22
2008026992

Printed and bound in Italy by Grafiche AZ, Verona, Italy
1 3 5 6 4 2

Marshall Cavendish Children

MARSHALL CAVENDISH CHILDREN

In Southern Italy where lemons and olives grow and lopsided donkeys pull cartloads of melons to market, there lived a famous general called Garibaldi. He had been far from home for many years, so when at last his ship sailed into port there was great excitement. His old friends cheered from the battlements, while Pecorino, their pet woodpecker, squawked loudly.

Aboard the ship were Garibaldi's wife, Anita, their four children, and his battle-weary soldiers. They had come home to fight the French army that had invaded Italy.

The French king came from the family of Bourbons that had ruled France since anyone could remember. So his soldiers were called Bourbons too.

Garibaldi was a fine figure of a man. Around his waist he wore a belt as wide as a footpath with a buckle as big as a pizza. In fact, it was a pizza. His army wore pizza buckles too. Fighting made them very hungry. It was then that they took off their pizza buckles and ate them, so their pantaloons would fall right down to their ankles. The soldiers wore bright red shirts and a good job too because they splashed tomato sauce everywhere when they ate their pizzas.

"How are my grandparents?" Garibaldi asked his old friends. They shook their heads. "The Bourbon army ransacked their lovely farmhouse and stole all their food. They have taken shelter in that funny stone hut in the olive grove."

As they approached the stone hut, they could smell Grandmother's delicious soup wafting towards them. Much hugging and kissing went on. Garibaldi threw his grandmother into the air with delight. The soldiers fell upon the soup and ate it all up.

"You're as bad as the Bourbons," scolded Grandmother, knocking one of the soldiers playfully on the head with her ladle, though secretly she was pleased that they liked her cooking so much.

"Before we can tackle the Bourbons, we need sleep," said Anita wisely. "There will be room for us all at your grandparents' old farmhouse." And so Garibaldi, Anita, his children and his soldiers returned to the farmhouse and settled down for the night.

Garibaldi dreamed of bringing peace to Italy. Anita dreamed of peace for the whole world. The children dreamed of fun and games, and the soldiers dreamed of pizzas.

Meanwhile back at the little stone hut, the smell of cooking had attracted the Bourbons. Stealthily they crept forward in the hope of finding something to eat, but the soup had gone.

Desperate with hunger, the Bourbons woke the old couple and dragged them away to cook for them. Luckily Pecorino had seen them. He hitched up his droopy drawers and followed them to a ruined pigeon house in the middle of a flat plain. Pecorino flew back to the farmhouse to raise the alarm.

Garibaldi roused everyone and ordered his soldiers to prepare for battle. "Hold on to your pantaloons and buckle up!" he cried.

Anita hid the children in an old barrel for safety and joined the army with her sword between her teeth.

The army marched out of the farmhouse, their trousers firmly held up by their pizza belts. Pecorino led the way from the top of the flagpole. As Garibaldi shouted "CHARGE!" his army surged forward, wielding their water balloons.

The battle waged for hours and hours and hours. Garibaldi's men fought so hard and got so hungry that soon all the pizzas had been eaten. Their pantaloons fell down, first to their knees and then to their ankles.

As the Bourbons sank to the ground groaning in their defeat, Garibaldi declared victory, and raised his balloon above his head.

Anita and the grandparents now felt sorry for the defeated Bourbons.

"I'll make them some biscuits!" said Grandmother.

She despatched Garibaldi's children to retrieve the ingredients that, under the very noses of the Bourbons, she had hidden in the farmhouse – eggs, butter, flour and sugar – and with a flourish she produced from her skirt pocket a large bar of chocolate.
"We'll call them Bourbon biscuits!" she declared.

She made piles and piles of them, one for each Bourbon soldier, and even when all the chocolate was used up, she carried on making more and more biscuits.

Pecorino, cross that the chocolate had run out, pecked at the plain biscuits until they had holes all over them.

At first Grandmother was angry and then she had a wonderful idea. “Pecorino, fetch the grapes that have been drying on the vines and we’ll fill the holes with them.”

And, hey presto, another biscuit was born. “What are we going to call it this time?” asked Pecorino. Anita put her arm fondly round Garibaldi’s waist. “We’ll name it after the apple of my eye! We’ll call it GARIBALDI’s biscuit!”

Garibaldi ordered the biscuits to be carried to the old farmhouse. Everyone was invited and sat together round the big wooden table.

Grandmother had insisted on making more soup, gallons of it, helped by the Bourbons who collected the herbs and vegetables.

When everyone had eaten their fill, there was enough soup left over to boil up all the soldiers's pantaloons, their socks and Pecorino's droopy drawers too. When they were dry, they were so stiff that both armies stood straight and tall and nobody's trousers ever fell down again. Pecorino couldn't even get into his pantaloons, so for ever after he flew naked and showed off his fine feathers.

In Italy people still talk proudly about Garibaldi and his men as the bravest army that ever lived, and Grandmother's Garibaldi biscuits are eaten to this day.

GARIBALDI

Giuseppe Garibaldi was a sensitive boy who cried when he accidentally hurt the leg of a grasshopper. There are many conflicting stories about him, but it is known that he had lived for a time in Montevideo in Uruguay. He rescued a Brazilian beauty, Anita Riberas, from marriage to a man she did not love. They eloped and together had many adventures and battles in South America on land and at sea. They had four children and in 1848 sailed back to Garibaldi's homeland of Italy. With them came his "Italian Legion," who were Italian exiles. They wore red woollen shirts, which had been bought cheaply from a merchant in Montevideo. They were popularly referred to as Garibaldinis.

Garibaldi's great achievement was to unite Italy. By challenging the power of Rome and insisting that Italy belonged to the people, he was adored by his army and feared by the French. The Garibaldinis were a match for any tyrant.

“All history is a delightful fantasy,” declared Voltaire, “and, er, Garibaldi’s Biscuit is living proof of that!”

The Garibaldi biscuit was first manufactured by the London biscuit company Peek Freans in 1861. It was named after Giuseppe Garibaldi, who was hailed as a hero when he visited England a few years later. The biscuits have remained popular ever since, despite being referred to rather unflatteringly by some people as “dead fly biscuits,” because they are baked using squashed currants sandwiched between the two thin layers of biscuit.

The Bourbon biscuit is also a sandwich, consisting of two thin, rectangular layers of dark chocolate biscuit with a chocolate fondant filling. It too was originally manufactured by Peek Freans in London, but it didn't appear until much later in 1910. Its origin was lost in the mists of time until this book revealed the true course of events that unfolded on the plains outside the medieval town of Oria in Puglia, and clarified the important role played by Garibaldi's Grandmother in the creation of the biscuits.

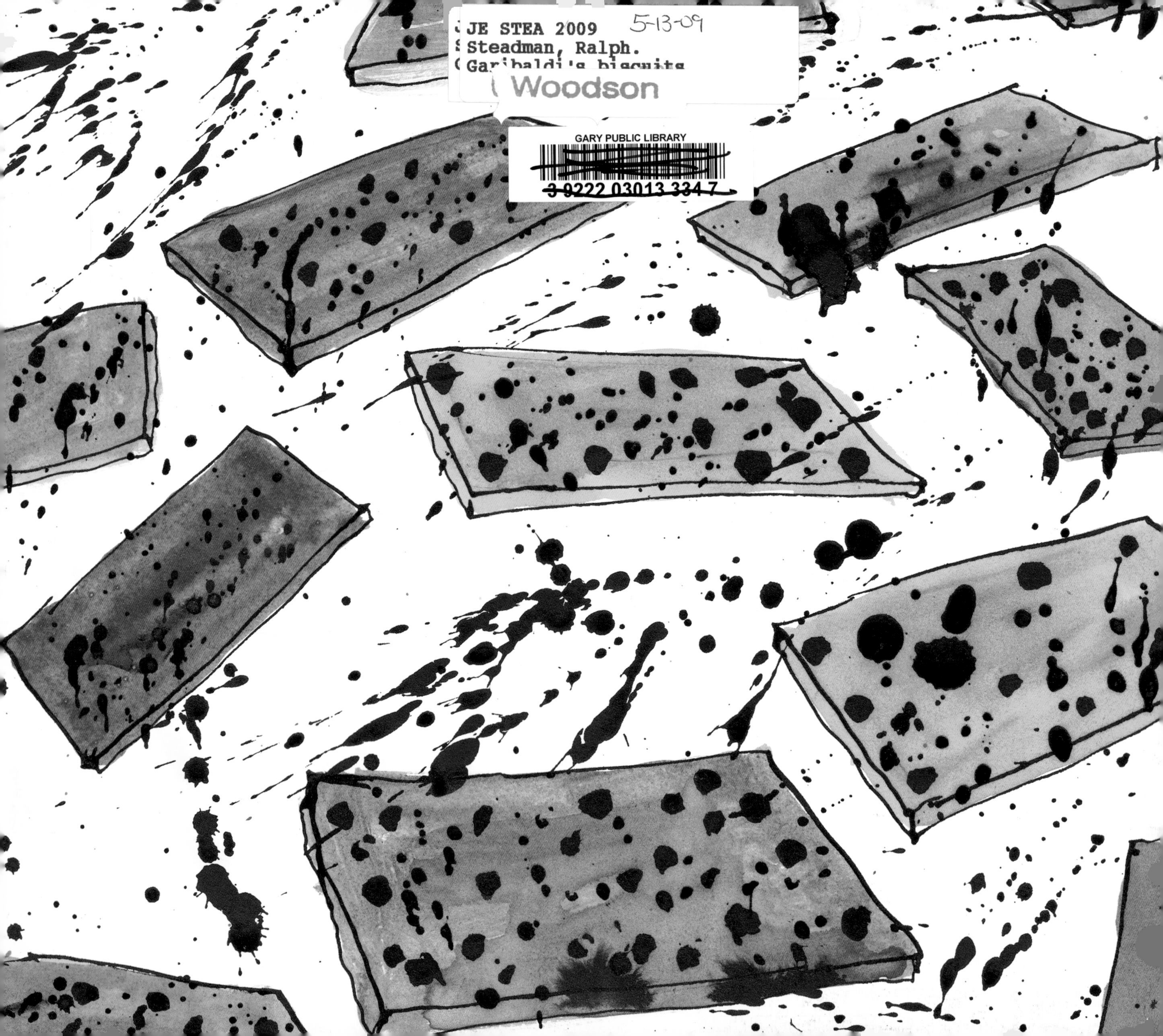